FRANKENSTEIN

FRANKENSTEIN

MONSTER Chronicles

STEPHEN KRENSKY

Lerner Publications Company · Minneapolis

Lerner Publications Company
A division of Lerner Publishing Group
241 First Avenue North
Minneapolis, MN 55401 U.S.A.

Website address: www.lernerbooks.com

Library of Congress Cataloging-in-Publication Data

Krensky, Stephen.
    Frankenstein / by Stephen Krensky.
        p.   cm. — (Monster chronicles)
    Includes bibliographical references and index.
    ISBN-13: 978-0-8225-5923-8 (lib. bdg. : alk. paper)
    ISBN-10: 0-8225-5923-4 (lib. bdg. : alk. paper)
        1. Shelley, Mary Wollstonecraft, 1797-1851. Frankenstein—Juvenile literature.
    2. Shelley, Mary Wollstonecraft, 1797-1851—Adaptations—Juvenile literature.
    3. Frankenstein films—History and criticism—Juvenile literature.
    4. Frankenstein (Fictitious character)—Juvenile literature. 5. Monsters in
    literature—Juvenile literature. I. Title.
    PR5397.F73K74 2007
    823'.7—dc22   2005024453

Manufactured in the United States of America
1 2 3 4 5 6 - JR - 12 11 10 09 08 07

TABLE OF CONTENTS

1 A Stitch in Time...

It was a dark and stormy night. Or maybe it wasn't, not really. But when you think of Frankenstein, that's the kind of weather that comes to mind. No bright sunshine. No chirping birds. No rainbows. Instead, there is thunder and

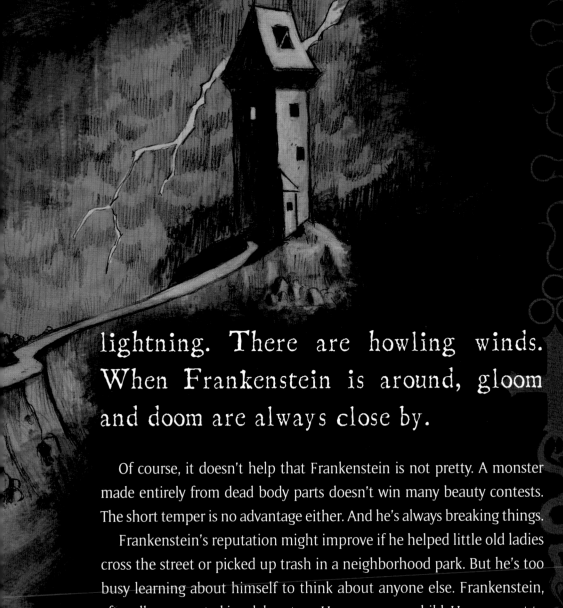

lightning. There are howling winds. When Frankenstein is around, gloom and doom are always close by.

Of course, it doesn't help that Frankenstein is not pretty. A monster made entirely from dead body parts doesn't win many beauty contests. The short temper is no advantage either. And he's always breaking things.

Frankenstein's reputation might improve if he helped little old ladies cross the street or picked up trash in a neighborhood park. But he's too busy learning about himself to think about anyone else. Frankenstein, after all, was created in a laboratory. He was never a child. He never got to make little mistakes and learn from them. He never went to school or played sports in the backyard. No, he had to start out as a grown-up monster and take it from there. All he really wants is a life of his own. But a monster that wants a life of his own is definitely heading for trouble.

But is this really fair? Is Frankenstein truly a bad guy? Sure, he's a monster—there's no getting around that. Still, as monsters go, he could be worse. He doesn't suck people's blood like a vampire or destroy entire cities like Godzilla. He doesn't rip people apart like a werewolf or burn villages to a crisp like some wandering dragon.

So why do we give him such a hard time? Well, the main thing is all those stitches. There's the general impression that he's a dead person brought back to life. But this is not strictly true. He's actually parts of several dead people sewn together and brought back to life.

Frankenstein, like vampires and ghosts, belongs to a long monster tradition of dead things coming back to life. That's what makes them so scary. Humans, it seems, prefer dead things to stay dead.

WOULD TWO HEADS BE BETTER THAN ONE?

The idea of mixing and matching body parts has been around for a long time. In ancient Greek mythology, for example, the Minotaur was a man with the head of a bull. True, he did not have the best reputation (he liked to eat helpless young men and women). And he was kept a prisoner in a stone maze called a labyrinth. But still . . . nobody

Some mixed creatures in Greek myths, such as the half-man and half-horse centaurs, were warriors and heroes.

The Egyptian god Ra *(above, right)* has a falcon's head on a man's body. In this tomb painting, Ra performs a ritual on a mummy *(left)*.

made fun of the Minotaur or tried to burn him alive.

Then there was the sun god Ra from Egypt. Ra had a falcon's head on a man's body, but nobody seemed to mind. In fact, many Egyptian gods and goddesses had animal heads. Lions, jackals,

rams, hawks, cats—all sat on the shoulders of men or women. And these heads and bodies served the Egyptians well—at least for a few thousand years.

Mix-and-match animals have also drawn a fair measure of respect. In ancient Greek stories, the chimera was a fire-breathing creature with a lion's head, a goat's body, and a serpent's tail. This is a pretty strange combination. But you don't see people laughing at chimeras. And what about griffins? They have the head and wings of an eagle mounted on the body of a lion. Eagles and lions are both royal creatures, but that doesn't mean a creature containing parts of both will work out. And yet the griffin pulled it off.

In Greek myth, griffins belonged to the god Zeus. Later, they appeared as gargoyles—scary-looking spouts—on gutters of churches in medieval Europe.

Of course, these creatures mingled various animal parts. But there was one important distinction—they weren't *dead* animal parts.

In Jewish legend, a golem is a creature made of clay and brought to life by a mystical spell. Golems were meant to help with household chores. But sometimes golems got other ideas and caused trouble. (Frankenstein would have understood.)

Minotaurs, chimeras, and griffins were perfectly normal, at least to the people who believed in them. They weren't dug up in graveyards in the middle of the night. They weren't stitched together in a laboratory and shocked into life by bolts of lightning. And fairly or not, maybe that makes all the difference.

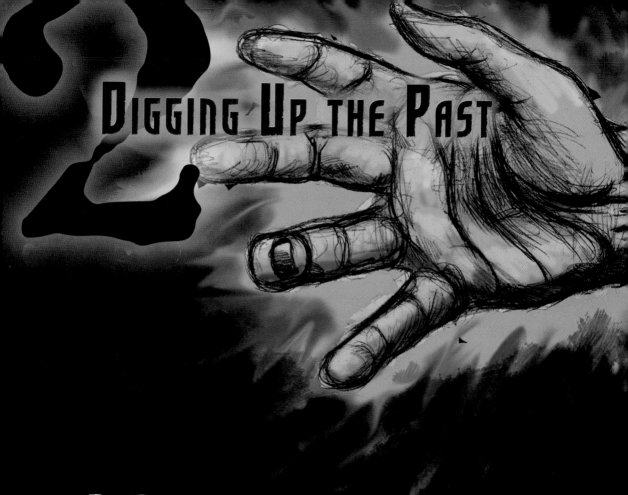

2 Digging Up the Past

Much of the blame for Frankenstein's reputation starts with a writer named Mary Shelley. This makes perfect sense. After all, she created the monster in the first place, in her 1818 novel *Frankenstein, or the Modern Prometheus.*

But Shelley did not call him Frankenstein. His name was Adam—a biblical reference to the first man God created. In the novel, Adam was known as Frankenstein's monster. Frankenstein actually referred to Victor Frankenstein, the doctor who created Adam.

Dr. Frankenstein and his monster are tragic figures, and so was their creator. Shelley was born Mary Godwin in London, England, in 1797. Her life had a sad beginning, as her mother died just days after Mary's birth. When her father remarried a few years later, Mary didn't like her new stepmother at all. And her stepmother felt much the same way

Mary Shelley loved literature and philosophy. She also enjoyed a new type of popular fiction called Gothic novels. They were dark stories of ghosts, family curses, and crumbling castles.

about Mary. All this sounds like a Cinderella story, and it is—except that young Mary had no fairy god-mother to rescue her.

Mary did not go to school, but she spent a lot of time reading books and writing stories. Then, at sixteen, she fell in love with a twenty-one-year-old poet named Percy Bysshe Shelley. He was already fa-mous, and he was already married (although he and his wife were no longer liv-ing together). Mary's father told her that the relationship must stop at once. Did Mary listen? No. Instead, she packed up and left with Percy for Switzerland in 1816.

Mary's parents, William Godwin and Mary Wollstonecraft, were both well known themselves. Godwin was a philosopher and writer. Wollstonecraft was also a writer and an early champion of women's rights.

Lord Byron rented Villa Diodati on the shores of Lake Geneva in Switzerland for the summer of 1816.

CREATING SOMETHING FROM NOTHING

Among their friends in Switzerland was the English poet Lord Byron. One night Mary and Percy were sitting with Byron and another friend, John Polidari. It was a dark and stormy night, so Byron suggested that they each make up a horror story.

Nineteen-year-old Mary could have been intimidated at the thought. After all, Percy and Byron were both famous poets, and Polidari was an educated physician. But she wasn't discouraged. In fact, she gave the challenge more thought than the others did.

May 1816 began the coldest, wettest, and darkest summer on record in Europe. Tons of dust from a volcanic eruption in faraway Indonesia drifted in the atmosphere. The dust reduced sunlight and caused weather changes around the world. In Switzerland the fog and frequent storms provided a gloomy backdrop for Lord Byron's horror-story challenge.

"I busied myself to think of a story," she later remembered "a story to rival those who had excited me to the task. One which would speak to the mysterious fears of our nature, and awaken thrilling horror—one to make the reader dread to look around, to curdle the blood, and quicken the beatings of the heart."

But where to start? Maybe electricity would provide her with the right spark she needed. She remembered that during the 1790s, an Italian doctor named Luigi Galvani had used electricity to jolt the muscles of dead frogs. The muscles had twitched in response to the charge. How could this be? Had Galvani mysteriously brought the muscles back to life? If this could be done for a muscle, could it be done for a whole animal? What about a whole person? No one had yet accomplished this feat, but that didn't mean it couldn't be done.

Were such thoughts crazy? Early nineteenth-century scientists couldn't say. Electricity was still a fairly new discovery. It was marveled at, something magical with unknown properties. Could it bring someone back to life? Well, anything was possible. (And keep in mind that electricity remains a powerful tool in modern medicine. Medical defibrillators bring many patients back from the brink of death after their hearts have failed during heart attacks.)

Closer to home, Mary had lost an infant daughter who had been born prematurely. But she had dreamed that the girl had been brought back to life. She knew that her baby was gone, but still. . . . And then one night, her imagination revealed a scene to her. "I saw—with shut eyes, but acute mental vision—I saw the pale student of unhallowed [unholy] arts kneeling beside the thing he had put together. I saw the hideous

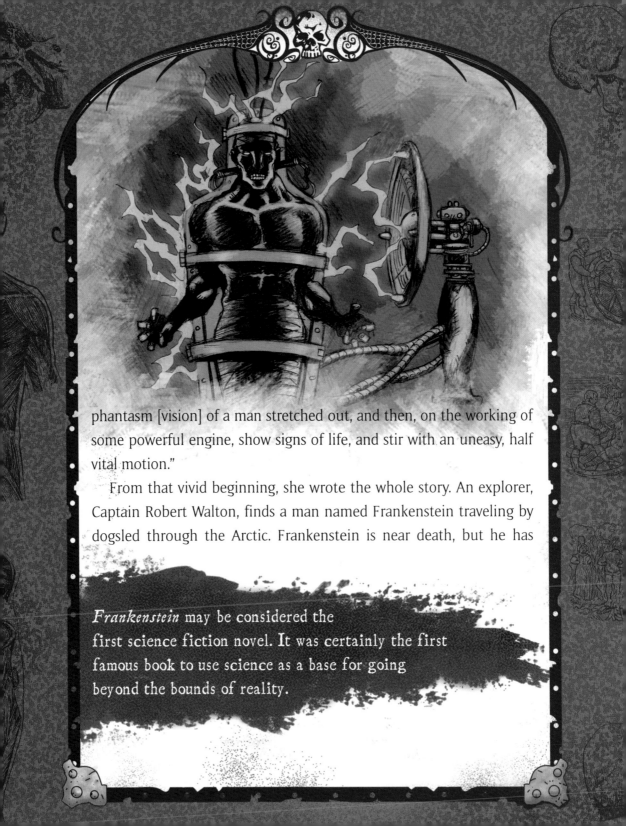

phantasm [vision] of a man stretched out, and then, on the working of some powerful engine, show signs of life, and stir with an uneasy, half vital motion."

From that vivid beginning, she wrote the whole story. An explorer, Captain Robert Walton, finds a man named Frankenstein traveling by dogsled through the Arctic. Frankenstein is near death, but he has

Frankenstein may be considered the first science fiction novel. It was certainly the first famous book to use science as a base for going beyond the bounds of reality.

quite a tale to tell. He explains that he had created a new human being from different parts of dead people. His hope had been to create a perfect human, but he failed. And the creature had turned out so deformed that Frankenstein had run away from it.

The monster is alive, though. He wanders around the countryside looking for friendship. But his appearance works against him. His yellow skin is stretched thin to cover his muscles. His black hair and white teeth seem straightforward enough, but his shriveled complexion and black lips are hard to ignore. People react in horror. It's hard not to be scared at the sight of such a creature.

In his bitterness, the monster seeks revenge against his creator. He kills Victor Frankenstein's younger brother and later finds Frankenstein again. The monster is lonely and wants a companion. Out of fear, Frankenstein agrees to create a bride for the monster. But later he changes his mind. Not surprisingly, this angers the monster. He kills Frankenstein's wife, Elizabeth, and his close friend Henry Clerval. Now it's Frankenstein who's angry. He plans to pursue the monster to his death. But Dr. Frankenstein is the one who dies. The monster, however, appears to Captain Walton and explains his side of the story. At the end, the monster leaves Walton to travel toward the North Pole, expecting death to catch up soon.

> Mary Shelley wrote six other novels, some travel books, and other works. She died in 1851.

Victor Frankenstein was based on Percy Bysshe Shelley. The name Frankenstein may come from Castle Frankenstein in Germany, which Mary Shelley may have visited a few years before writing her novel.

THE STORY TAKES ON A LIFE OF ITS OWN

Mary Shelley's story was much more than a parlor game. She turned it into a novel worthy of publication. It's not the happiest story, but of course it wasn't meant to be. And the biggest mystery in the plot, which is how Dr. Frankenstein actually brings the monster to life, is not

explained. All Shelley tells us is that Dr. Frankenstein endures "day and nights of incredible . . . fatigue."

The public reaction to *Frankenstein, or the Modern Prometheus* was generally favorable. It was published anonymously at first, without Mary Shelley's name. So, many readers assumed a man had written it.

In ancient Greek and Roman myths, the gods give Prometheus (*below*) the task of creating humans. But he is eventually punished by the gods for overstepping his bounds. Shelley compared Dr. Frankenstein to Prometheus.

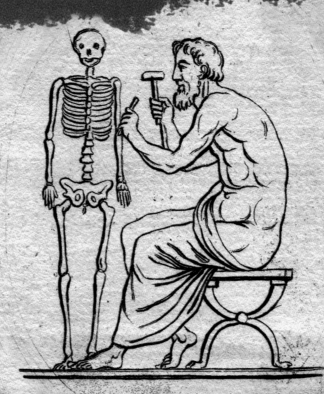

(In those days, publishers rarely published the work of women writers.) Over time, though, the author's identity became known, and for the 1831 edition, she wrote an introduction. In it she acknowledged the question that everyone had been asking since the book had first appeared: "How I, then a young girl, came to think of . . . such a hideous idea?"

Mary didn't really answer the question. (She enjoyed being a little mysterious.) But hideous or not, the idea survived. Mary had four children with Shelley, but only one lived to adulthood. Of all her children, real and literary, Frankenstein alone made a lasting impression.

3 FRANKENSTEIN STEPS OUT

It didn't take long for *Frankenstein*'s characters to escape from the printed page. Only a few years after the book's original publication, Mary Shelley herself sat in a London theater audience watching a play based on her work. It was called *Presumption, or the Fate of Frankenstein*. And this was just the beginning.

Various versions of the story turned up in theaters throughout the 1800s. Good or bad, they all kept the idea of Frankenstein and his monster very much alive in the public mind.

A scene from *Frankenstein, or the Model Man* plays on a London stage in 1850.

A poster advertises the original Frankenstein movie released by Edison Films in 1910.

And then, in the twentieth century, came motion pictures. Thomas Edison, the inventor of this new film technology and the owner of one of the first movie studios, produced the first Frankenstein film in 1910. It was ten minutes long. That wasn't a lot of time to tell the whole story. So the movie concentrated on one thing—the monster attacking Victor Frankenstein on his wedding night. This monster was a hairy, twisted figure. The audience wasn't supposed to feel sorry for him. They were just supposed to scream. And they did.

A 1927 stage version of *Frankenstein* switched the first names of the characters of Victor Frankenstein and his friend Henry Clerval. This change was followed in most of the later Frankenstein movies.

A Star Is Born

During the next twenty years, two more Frankenstein movies were made. Neither was a big success. But the fourth one was different. In 1931 director James Whale took a different approach. His monster would be someone the audience sympathized with—even while he horrified them.

The role of the monster in Whale's film was first offered to actor Bela Lugosi. He had triumphed

Whale's version of *Frankenstein* was produced by Universal Pictures. Universal was fast becoming a leader in a new type of cinema—the horror movie. The studio had already produced three creepy classics: *The Hunchback of Notre Dame* (1923), *The Phantom of the Opera* (1925), and *Dracula* (1931).

playing the vampire Dracula on film less than a year before. But Lugosi didn't think much of Frankenstein's monster. In Shelley's novel, the monster has a voice. He has his own story to tell. In the movie script, the monster didn't even speak. He just groaned and grunted. He wasn't an absolutely evil creature in the movie, but much of his humanity had been removed. It was, Lugosi thought, no part for a real actor.

Forty-three-year-old Boris Karloff politely disagreed. He was a character actor used to playing small parts. He wasn't the big star Lugosi was. But Karloff recognized something special in what he called "the dear old Monster." He insisted that this "was a pathetic creature who, like us all, had neither wish nor say in his creation and certainly did not wish upon itself the hideous image which automatically terrified humans whom it tried to befriend." With that kind of perspective, it's no wonder Karloff got the part.

In a scene from *Frankenstein* (1931), Henry Frankenstein (Colin Clive), *left*, and his assistant Fritz (Dwight Frye), *right*, prepare to bring the monster to life.

At the beginning of *Frankenstein*, Dr. Frankenstein's assistant, the hunchbacked Fritz, is stealing a brain from the local medical college. (This will be the brain that Dr. Frankenstein inserts in his new man.) There are two brains available in jars—one is normal and one is the brain of a criminal. Fritz intends to take the normal brain. But at the last moment, the sound of a gong startles him. He drops the normal brain, and the jar smashes on the floor. The brain is ruined. Terrified, Fritz grabs the abnormal brain and scampers off.

This is not good news. Everyone knows that the movie will go badly for the monster. Everyone but Dr. Frankenstein. Unaware of Fritz's substitution, he starts out with high hopes.

Digging Around for Ideas

During their medical training, doctors study human anatomy by dissecting cadavers (dead bodies). Modern medical schools use legally donated cadavers, but this was not always the case. Centuries ago in England, the law allowed doctors to experiment only on the bodies of dead criminals. But there weren't enough dead criminals to go around. So doctors resorted to making nighttime raids on cemeteries to steal the fresh corpses they needed.

In 1931's *Frankenstein*, Henry Frankenstein and Fritz dig up a corpse in a graveyard *(below)*. They then steal another dead body from the gallows (wooden frames from which criminals were hanged). These corpses, along with the brain Fritz steals from a medical college, become the raw material for Dr. Frankenstein's experiment.

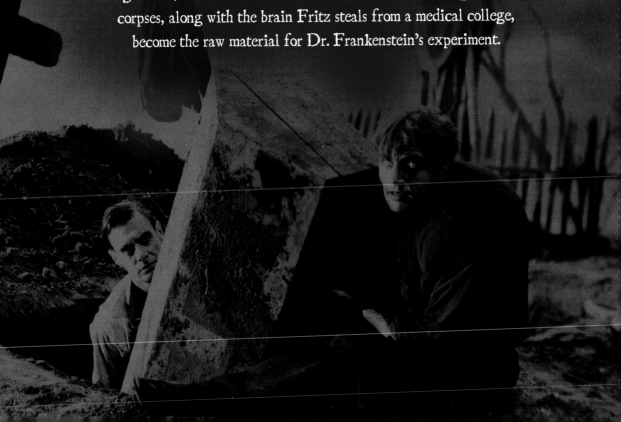

"You really believe that you can bring life to the dead?" asks Dr. Frankenstein's mentor, Dr. Waldman.

"That body is not dead," Dr. Frankenstein insists. "It has never lived. I created it! I made it with my own hands, from the bodies I took from graves, from gallows, from anywhere."

Still, he's not exactly sure what will happen. But at the crucial moment in his laboratory, the monster stirs.

"It's moving," gasps Dr. Frankenstein. "It's alive . . . It's alive . . . It's alive!"

The costume Boris Karloff wore in *Frankenstein* (1931) weighed more than forty pounds. It was very hot to wear during filming.

Alive, but not destined for happiness. By the movie's end, the monster has terrorized Dr. Frankenstein, his friends, and the nearby villagers. They pursue the monster to an old windmill. There he appears to die a fiery death, pinned to the floor by a mighty beam.

But fiery deaths can be misleading, especially when a movie does well. Critics gave *Frankenstein*'s premiere good reviews in the newspapers, and audiences were strongly affected. Unlike the movie *Dracula*, which had

Frankenstein's monster has no name in the movie *Frankenstein* (unlike in the book, where his name is Adam). This makes him seem less like a real person.

only been a commercial success, *Frankenstein* made several movie critics' top-ten lists that year. Awards are nice, but much to the delight of the producer, Universal Studios, *Frankenstein* also made twice as much money as *Dracula*.

TRUE LOVE IS HARD TO FIND

The movie studio naturally wanted a sequel to the successful *Frankenstein* original. In 1935 Universal released *The Bride of Frankenstein*. It again featured Karloff as the monster, with English actress Elsa Lanchester as his bride-to-be. The action picks up exactly where the first movie left off, in the smoldering ruins of the windmill. Here we discover that the monster was not turned to toast after all. He was saved by falling into a well that lay below the windmill. This is good news for him, but not so good for Dr. Frankenstein, who has also barely survived. The monster manages to cause a lot of trouble before reaching a short period of peace living with a blind hermit. (The hermit is not frightened of the monster because he cannot see him.) The monster is soon discovered by hunters, though, and forced to flee again.

A scene from *The Bride of Frankenstein* (1935). They're two of a kind, but the bride (Elsa Lanchester), *left*, is not happy with her new husband (Boris Karloff), *right*.

In the meantime, Dr. Frankenstein's old teacher, Dr. Praetorius, is badgering him. Praetorius wants him to resume making new people from old body parts. Dr. Frankenstein refuses at first. But then Praetorius and the monster join forces and kidnap Dr. Frankenstein's wife, Elizabeth. So Dr. Frankenstein changes his mind. Together, Praetorius and Dr. Frankenstein create a bride for the monster—or so they think. But when she comes to life, the unexpected happens. She is as repulsed by Frankenstein's monster as everyone else. In his

The monster learns to talk in *The Bride of Frankenstein*. Being able to speak was handy for the plot. But, unfortunately, it did not help the monster in the end.

despair, the monster tells Dr. Frankenstein to leave. He then destroys the laboratory (and Dr. Praetorius) in a massive explosion.

Even though both *The Bride of Frankenstein* and *Frankenstein* are horror movies, *Bride* is sadder because we get to know the monster better. We see him trying desperately to overcome his plight. But fate does not treat him kindly. So when that explosion comes, it seems that Frankenstein is finished at last. But really, he's just getting started.

4 FRANKENSTEIN GETS EVEN BIGGER

The success of *Frankenstein* and *The Bride of Frankenstein* was the best sign that the monster was not dead—at least not permanently. Dr. Frankenstein might have regretted making his creature, but Universal Studios never did. And the

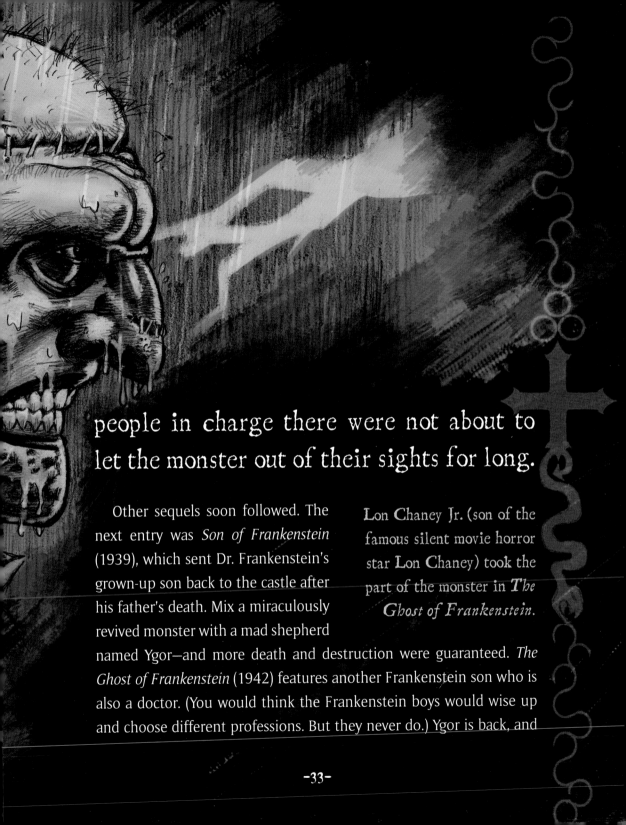

people in charge there were not about to
let the monster out of their sights for long.

Other sequels soon followed. The
next entry was *Son of Frankenstein*
(1939), which sent Dr. Frankenstein's
grown-up son back to the castle after
his father's death. Mix a miraculously
revived monster with a mad shepherd

Lon Chaney Jr. (son of the
famous silent movie horror
star Lon Chaney) took the
part of the monster in *The
Ghost of Frankenstein.*

named Ygor—and more death and destruction were guaranteed. *The
Ghost of Frankenstein* (1942) features another Frankenstein son who is
also a doctor. (You would think the Frankenstein boys would wise up
and choose different professions. But they never do.) Ygor is back, and

so is the monster. Throw in another mad scientist, a brain transplant, and a laboratory inferno, and the film was in business.

Frankenstein moved outside this established formula in *Frankenstein Meets the Wolf Man* (1943). Here the monster gets to know another monster outcast—in this case a werewolf. These two hunted

It's bad temper versus hairiness in this battle between Bela Lugosi's Frankenstein, *left*, and Lon Chaney Jr's Wolf Man, *right*. In *Frankenstein Meets the Wolf Man* (1943), Universal Pictures brought together its two most popular horror-movie characters.

monsters are both scorned by society. Can they get along with each other? No, because the plot relies on them being enemies rather than friends.

If two monsters were good, then three would be even better. That's the premise behind *House of Frankenstein* (1944), which manages to cram Frankenstein, the Wolf Man, and Dracula into its plot. In the end, Frankenstein sinks in a bog, where he is brought down by quicksand as well as by a feverish plot.

CRACKING SMILES INSTEAD OF BONES

After so much death and destruction, Frankenstein was ready for a change. In 1948 the monster lumbered into comedy in *Abbott and Costello Meet Frankenstein.* Abbott and Costello were a comedy team whose movie plots often placed them in dire straits. Bud Abbott was the tall, reasonable, serious figure in their routines. Lou Costello was the short, round, silly one.

As dire straits go, meeting Frankenstein is about as dire as straits get. A beautiful woman doctor who works for Dracula plans to take Lou's brain and place it in the Frankenstein monster. The Wolf Man is here, too, and even the Invisible Man (or at least his voice) makes a brief appearance. Lou escapes in the end, but the monsters are not so lucky. (Then again, they almost never are.)

Frankenstein's tragic end in horror films seemed inevitable. But he had better luck elsewhere. He inspired a hit record single, "The Monster Mash," which, in its words, was a "graveyard smash" in 1962. Bobby "Boris" Pickett sang the song in an easily recognized Boris

Karloff imitation. The catchy tune showed a fun side of Frankenstein that had not been previously observed.

"The Monster Mash," by Bobby "Boris" Pickett, hit number one on the music charts in October 1962. It became a Halloween standard and has sold almost four million copies over the years.

Playing Frankenstein for laughs was also the basis for *The Munsters*, a television series that ran from 1964 to 1966. Herman Munster, a Frankenstein look-alike, was the father of a very unusual family. His wife, Lily, and father-in-law, Grandpa, were vampires (although not very bloodthirsty ones). His young son, Eddie, was growing up to be a werewolf. His niece Marilyn, however, was an attractive, young blond woman (who naturally was a great embarrassment to the family).

Television's Herman Munster was the most cheerful character inspired by the Frankenstein story. He was also the only Frankenstein monster who laughed (something he did with earth-shattering regularity).

What was most interesting about this twist on the Frankenstein story was that the Munsters didn't live in a distant castle. They lived on an ordinary suburban American street. Many of their problems were the same as those of other sitcom families.

Young Frankenstein (1974) is a comedy, too, but this movie returns the monster to his traditional creepy village castle. This film is the brainchild of Mel Brooks, who cowrote and directed it. It honors the Frankenstein movies of the past and makes fun of them at the same time. And in a rare treat for the monster, he finally gets a happy ending (marriage and a successful business).

Perhaps the most faithful to the book of the Frankenstein movies was *Mary Shelley's Frankenstein* (1994). English actor Kenneth Branagh directed the film and stars as Dr. Frankenstein. Robert de Niro took the role of the monster. De Niro,

In *Young Frankenstein* (1974), Marty Feldman *(below)* plays Dr. Frankenstein's wild-eyed assistant Igor. Sent to a lab to steal a brain for the monster, Igor misreads a warning label on the brain of an insane criminal. He thinks it's a healthy brain from someone named Abby Normal.

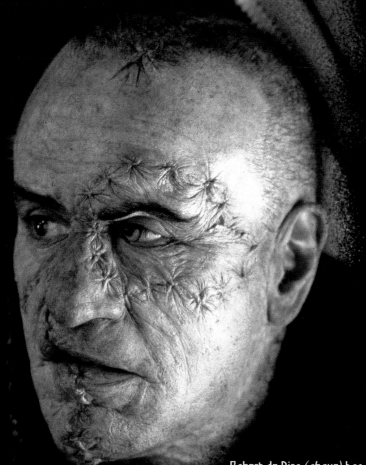

probably best known for playing gangsters, might not seem like an obvious choice for the role. But he made the monster more subdued and complex. The monster is truly a tortured soul and appears more human by not being as exaggerated a creature as earlier monsters.

Echoes of Frankenstein can also be found in the character of Data from *Star Trek: The Next Generation*. Data is an android, a computer built to resemble a human. One of Data's ongoing wishes is to feel human emotions—to achieve a sense of humanity he believes he lacks.

Data has the advantage of being perfectly presentable. (His pasty skin color and yellow eyes are a bit unusual, but in the multi-species world of the twenty-fourth century, he fits right in.) This no doubt was helpful in advancing his career with Starfleet.

More recently, *Van Helsing* (2004) again reunites Frankenstein with Dracula and the Wolf Man, although here the monster is working for Dracula. Frankenstein never seems destined to be the brains of the gang. It would probably help if he took on Dracula's fancy accent

Frankenstein, played by Shuler Hensley, *right*, appeared in *Van Helsing* (2004). The monster ends up joining forces with vampire hunter Van Helsing (Hugh Jackman), *center*, and monk-inventor Carl (David Wenham), *left*.

and formal clothes. The movie may not be his finest moment, but at least he's still finding work.

STAKING OUT NEW TERRITORY

Overall, Frankenstein has a lot to be proud of. The monster is one of the few fictional characters whose name has leaped outside his story to enter our everyday vocabulary. This rare group includes Scrooge from the novel *A Christmas Carol* and Romeo from the play *Romeo and Juliet*. To call someone a Scrooge is to say that the person is a miser, or a penny-pincher. A Romeo, on the other hand, is a romantic young lover. But Frankenstein has staked out a wider territory. Anything well intentioned that gets out of hand can be referred to as a Frankenstein monster.

Frankenstein has even lent his name to the ongoing debate about genetically modified (GM) foods. To create GM foods, scientists change a plant or animal's genes. The changes give GM foods advantages over their unmodified counterparts. For example, scientists can alter tomato-plant genes so the fruit doesn't get mushy as it ripens. But not everyone likes the idea of GM foods. Tinkering with genes, they argue, is dangerous. Some GM opponents have labeled these altered products "frankenfoods." There are some things, they say, that science should keep its nose out of. No doubt they would have told Victor Frankenstein to find a different hobby than collecting body parts.

Since its first publication, *Frankenstein* has raised the question of whether science sometimes goes too far. In Mary Shelley's time, modern

The Frankenstein monster is featured as a cereal shape in Frankenberry cereal *(left)*. His friend Count Chocula has a cereal of his own.

science was just getting started. The limits of twenty-first century science are nowhere in sight. But if scientists have more power than ever, then the mistakes they make can get pretty big too. How far should science go? Is there a line that should not be crossed? People hold heated views on both sides, and there is room for further discussions. Just to be safe, though, it might be wise to avoid having those talks on dark and stormy nights.

Excerpt from Mary Shelley's *Frankenstein*

As a scientist, Victor Frankenstein looks for the secret of creating life. He stitches together his creature and, one rainy night, gets it to breathe and move its limbs. But after all his work, Victor is repelled by the creature. As he discovers in this passage, however, he cannot get away from the monster he has created.

I had worked hard for nearly two years, for the sole purpose of infusing life into an inanimate body. For this I had deprived myself of rest and health. [B]ut now that I had finished, the beauty of the dream vanished, and breathless horror and disgust filled my heart. Unable to endure the aspect of the being I had created, I rushed out of the room, and continued a long time traversing my bedchamber, unable to compose my mind to sleep. At length . . . I threw myself on the bed in my clothes, endeavouring to seek a few moments of forgetfulness. But it was in vain: I slept, indeed, but I was disturbed by the wildest dreams. . . . I started from my sleep with horror . . . when, by the dim and yellow light of the moon . . . I beheld the wretch—the miserable monster whom I had created. He held up the curtain of the bed; and his eyes, if eyes they may be called, were fixed on me. His jaws opened, and he muttered some inarticulate sounds, while a grin wrinkled his cheeks. He might have spoken, but I did not hear; one hand was stretched out, seemingly to detain me, but I escaped, and rushed down stairs. . . .

SOURCE NOTES

16 Mary Shelley, *Frankenstein, or the Modern Prometheus* (1831 edition; repr., Charlottesville: University of Virginia Library Electronic Text Center, http://etext.lib.virginia.edu/toc/modeng/public/SheFran.html, 1999), viii–ix.

16–17 Ibid., x.

20 *The Mary Shelley Reader*, ed. Betty T. Bennett and Charles E. Robinson (New York: Oxford University Press, 1990), 39.

21 Shelley, *Frankenstein*, v.

25 Gregory William Mank, *It's Alive! The Classic Cinema Saga of Frankenstein* (San Diego: A. S. Barnes & Company, 1981), 27.

25 Ibid., 26.

28 Ibid., 4.

42 Shelley, *Frankenstein*, 43–44.

SELECTED BIBLIOGRAPHY

Halliwell, Leslie. *The Dead that Walk: Dracula, Frankenstein, the Mummy and Other Favorite Movie Monsters*. New York: Continuum Publishing, 1986.

Mank, Gregory William. *It's Alive! The Classic Cinema Saga of Frankenstein*. San Diego: A. S. Barnes & Company, 1981.

Shelley, Mary. *The Essential Frankenstein*. Edited by Leonard Wolf. New York: Plume, 1993.

——. *Frankenstein*. Edited by Johanna M. Smith. Boston: Bedford/St. Martin's, 2000.

——. *The Mary Shelley Reader*. Edited by Betty T. Bennett and Charles E. Robinson. New York: Oxford University Press, 1990.

Sveblar, Gary J., and Susan Sveblar, eds. *We Belong Dead: Frankenstein on Film*. Baltimore: Midnight Marquee Press, Inc., 1997.

Tropp, Martin. *Mary Shelley's Frankenstein*. Boston: Houghton Mifflin, 1976.

FURTHER READING AND WEBSITES

Frankenstein: Mary Shelley's Dream

http://www.thebakken.org/Frankenstein/exhibit.htm

The Bakken Library and Museum explores the novel *Frankenstein*, the life and work of its creator Mary Shelley, and the scientific discoveries that inspired the tale. A photo of a recreation of Victor Frankenstein's laboratory provides links to the 1831 edition of Frankenstein, "Mary Shelley's Family Tree," "Late 18th Century Scientific and Medical Instruments," and other areas of interest.

Frankenstein: Penetrating the Secrets of Nature.

http://www.nlm.nih.gov/hmd/frankenstein/frankhome.html

The National Library of Medicine examines the nineteenth-century science behind the story of Dr. Frankenstein's monster. The site considers how people in Shelley's day viewed the new sciences of chemistry and electricity. It also looks at some modern-day parallels of the "Frankenstein Syndrome"—such as cloning, genetically modified food, and animal-to-human organ transplants.

Nichols, Joan Kane. *Mary Shelley: Frankenstein's Creator.* York Beach, ME: Conari Press, 1998. Nichols's biography looks at Mary Shelley as the creator of the first science fiction novel in English. She also looks at the character of the woman who ran away with a famous poet, wrote her first novel at nineteen, and lost all but one of her children. In her day, Shelley lived what most people considered to be a scandalous life. Nichols also considers the difficulties Shelley faced and the strength she had to overcome them.

Schildt, Christopher. *Frankenstein: The Legacy.* New York: Pocket Books, 2001. Schildt's novel brings Mary Shelley's monster into the twenty-first century. At the end of Shelley's novel, Victor Frankenstein pursues his monster through Russia and into the Arctic. Schildt picks up the story

two centuries later, as three scientists learn that an old ship has been found frozen in Arctic ice. Aboard the ship, they discover Victor Frankenstein's notebook and decide to recreate Frankenstein's experiment using modern science.

Shelley, Mary. *Frankenstein*. Adapted by Gary Reed. New York: Puffin Books, 2005. This graphic novel version of Shelley's classic story focuses on the rage and pain of Victor Frankenstein and his monster.

——. *Frankenstein*. New York: Pocket Books, 2004. Historical background, explanatory notes, a chronology of Shelley's life, and discussion questions accompany the text of Shelley's novel.

MOVIES AND TV

Abbott and Costello Meet Frankenstein. Universal City, CA: Universal Studios, 2001, DVD. Seventeen years after filming its first Frankenstein movie, Universal Studios was still making money from the franchise. In this 1948 comedy, Frankenstein terrorizes the misfit team of Bud Abbott and Lou Costello. Abbott and Costello are sent to deliver a couple of crates to MacDougal's House of Horrors. But inside they find real monsters—not only Frankenstein but also Count Dracula, the Wolf Man, and the Invisible Man. Many consider the movie to be the best of the era's "horror comedies." The DVD edition includes an entertaining commentary and still photos from the movie set.

The Bride of Frankenstein. Universal City, CA: Universal Studios, 2001, DVD. This 1935 film was a sequel to the very popular *Frankenstein*. Dr. Frankenstein (Colin Clive) agrees to create a bride to keep his lonely monster (Boris Karloff) company. English stage actress Elsa Lanchester plays Mary Shelley in the film's opening scenes, setting up the story of how Shelley decides to continue the Frankenstein saga. Lanchester then returns later in the movie as the title character—the original bridezilla—

hissing and shrieking under her now-famous streaked wig. This DVD edition includes an original documentary, *She's Alive! Creating the Bride of Frankenstein*. Also included are rare photos from the movie set and weblinks on the DVD-ROM.

Frankenstein. Universal City, CA: Universal Studios, 2001, DVD. This 1931 horror film stars Colin Clive as Dr. Frankenstein and Boris Karloff as the monster. Hollywood makeup artist Jack Pierce designed the monster's flat, stitched head, deep-set eyes, and scarred face—a look that became synonymous with Frankenstein. This DVD edition features a documentary on the making of the movie, commentary by film historian Rudy Behlmer, and a bonus short film, *Boo!*

The Munsters: The Complete First Season. Universal City, CA: Universal Studios, 2004, DVD. Get a glimpse at life inside 1313 Mockingbird Lane, home of Herman Munster and his unusual family. Herman's job at the funeral home, Grandpa's wayward science experiments, the family's fire-breathing pet named Spot, and Eddie the werewolf's attempt to fit in at school are all fodder for laughs in this classic sitcom. This DVD edition contains the pilot and thirty-eight episodes from the 1964–1965 season.

Young Frankenstein. Los Angeles: Twentieth Century Fox, 2001, DVD. Director Mel Brooks gathered a large cast of comedians for his affectionate spoof on classic horror movies. Serious scientist Frederick Frankenstein (Gene Wilder) is a reluctant heir to the "mad doctor" theories of his late father. But when the mysterious Fraü Blucher (Cloris Leachman) convinces Frederick to read his father's research, Frederick is inspired. Assisted by a bug-eyed handyman named Igor (Marty Feldman) and a pretty but dim villager named Inga (Terri Garr), Frederick conducts his own reanimation experiment. The result is a seven-foot monster (Peter Boyle), with the brain of a criminal, who only wants to be loved.

ABOUT THE AUTHOR

Stephen Krensky is the author of many fiction and nonfiction books for children, including titles in the On My Own Folklore series and *Vampires, Werewolves, Dragons, The Mummy,* and *Bigfoot.* When he isn't hunched over his computer, he makes school visits and teaches writing workshops. In his free time, he enjoys playing tennis and softball and reading books by other people. Krensky lives in Massachusetts with his wife, Joan, and their family.

PHOTO ACKNOWLEDGMENTS

The images in this book are used with the permission of: © Royalty-Free/CORBIS, pp. 2-3; © Erich Lessing/Art Resource, NY, p. 9; © Historical Picture Archive/CORBIS, p. 10; © Bettmann/CORBIS, pp. 14, 20; The Granger Collection, New York, pp. 15, 23; Courtesy of U.S. Dept. of the Interior, National Park Service, Edison National Historic Site, p. 24; Courtesy of Universal Studios Licensing, LLLP, pp. 26, 27, 28, 30, 34, 39; "Young Frankenstein" © Twentieth Century Fox. All rights reserved. Photo courtesy The Everett Collection, p. 37; "Mary Shelley's Frankenstein" © TriStar/JSB Productions, Inc. All Rights Reserved. Courtesy of Sony Pictures Entertainment, p. 38; © Sam Lund/Independent Picture Service, p. 41. Illustrations by Bill Hauser, pp. 1, 6-7, 12-13, 17, 18, 22-23, 32-33. All page backgrounds illustrated by Bill Hauser/Independent Picture Service.

Front Cover: Courtesy of Universal Studios Licensing, LLLP. Photo by © John Kobal Foundation/Hulton Archive/Getty Images.